DIGBY AND THE CONSTRUCTION CREW

Dig It, Digby!

Jodie Parachini

illustrated by
John Joven

Albert Whitman & Company
Chicago, Illinois

When Digby arrived
at his work site one day,

with fuel to the max
and his lunch stored away,

he greeted his friends,
all the loaders and rigs,
then he got down to business
and started to dig.

He lifted and hauled
from daybreak till night,
yet deep in his gears
he felt, "Something's not right!"

When building a building,
each truck has a role.
But Digby was bored
simply digging his hole.

"I'm sure that my work
could be so much more fun!
There must be a new way
to get the job done."

"What if I mixed up
this digging and dumping,

with bouncing and prancing
and rocking and jumping?"

So Digby decided
that he'd take a chance—
he plucked up his courage
and started to...

dance.

Although he was loaded
with metal and rubble,
when twirling about
he felt light as a bubble.

The trucks were amazed by the curious scene. "Hey look!" shouted Mack. "It's a dancing machine!"

"If a digger like Digby
can shimmy and jive,
then deep in our engines
we ALL have the drive!"

"Try it!" called Digby
as he flipped with a spin.
And it DID look like fun,
so the others joined in.

From the towering cranes
to the burly backhoes,
every truck on the lot
was seen striking a pose.

First Diggory jigged
while Lori hip-hopped.
Old Morris discoed
till the foreman yelled...

"STOP!"

The trucks looked embarrassed,
their taillights burned red.
Not a beep could be heard.
Digby quivered with dread.

"Our site," boomed the foreman,
"has rules to obey!"
(But when did the rules
mention tap or ballet?)

"These are our buildings,
our concrete, our streets.
How do you *dare*
try to dance without...

BEATS!"

OUT came the trumpets
and saxes and drums—
two dumper trucks picked,
and the bulldozer strummed.

Every dipstick and stick shift
was buzzing with sound

while the trucks linked their hitches
and frolicked around.

Mix it!

Grind it!

Lift and haul.

We're mighty trucks. We do it all!

Come on, gang.
Let's join the crew.

Today we're building something new!

"Bravo!" shouted Digby,
as trucks celebrated,

applauding the buildings
their groove had created.

Now Digby can DIG IT
and dance with delight
while trucks do the boogie
at each building site!

For my family. Dance, sing, play, act, knit, make art, and follow your dreams.—JP

To my wife, Ana. Thank you for letting me build this amazing life with you.—JJ

Library of Congress Cataloging-in-Publication data
is on file with the publisher.
Text copyright © 2022 by Jodie Parachini
Illustrations copyright © 2022 by Albert Whitman & Company
Illustrations by John Joven
First published in the United States of America in 2022 by Albert Whitman & Company
ISBN 978-0-8075-1587-7 (hardcover)
ISBN 978-0-8075-1588-4 (ebook)

Printed in China
10 9 8 7 6 5 4 3 2 1 WKT 26 25 24 23 22

Design by Rick DeMonico

For more information about Albert Whitman & Company,
visit our website at www.albertwhitman.com.